To Ran Tziper, who loved the dove.

# The
# Hawk
## and the
# Dove

**Paul Kor**

**Translated by Annette Appel**

Kids Can Press

The feisty hawk is feeling sad.
"No one likes me. Times are bad.
I don't want another war. I can't bear it anymore.
Everyone is blaming me, so I will change,
just wait and see."

Masking his face and putting
on gloves ...

The hawk becomes a gentle dove!

The entire land is filled with light —
A rainbow of colors, sunny and bright.

The soldiers dance and spread their cheer
To every city, far and near.

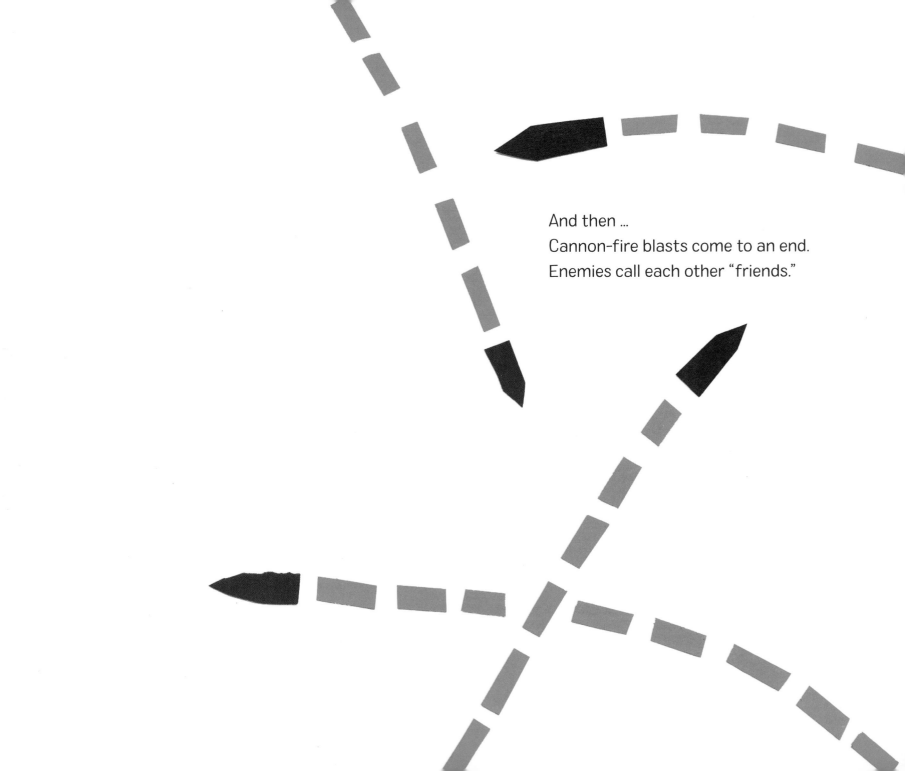

And then ...
Cannon-fire blasts come to an end.
Enemies call each other "friends."

The tank falls silent.
The battles cease.

The tractor hums a tune of peace.

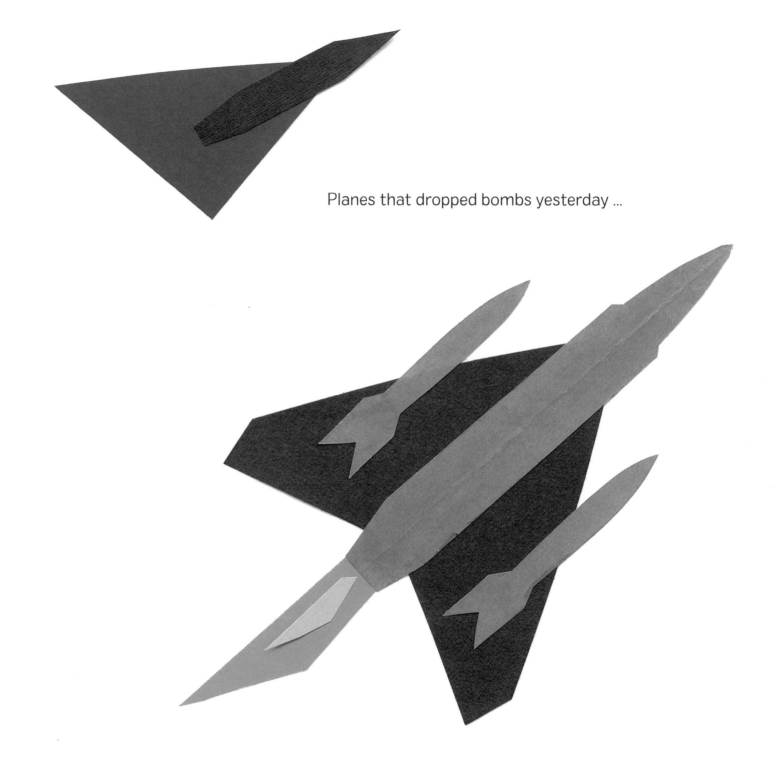

Planes that dropped bombs yesterday ...

A blanket of calm envelops the world,
Bringing joy to each boy and girl.

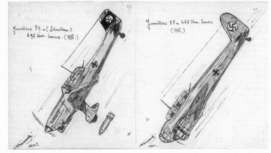

to depict the atmosphere of war and his sadness, anxiety and fear about the situation. He was a child in France during World War II, and he would sit for days drawing tanks, fighter planes and warships. Some of the paper cutouts in this book are reminiscent of the drawings from his childhood, a time that Paul described as happy until the war broke out.

However, Paul didn't complete *The Hawk and the Dove* until much later, during the 1982 Lebanon War. When the son of one of his good friends was killed in the conflict, Paul felt a need to return to his artwork and the book he had begun years before; he wanted to share its message of peace with the world. This time, he chose to paint the pictures, using aquarelle and colored pencils, and the book was published without the special cut-page design.

The book you are now holding in your hands is the story in its original form, as Paul first imagined it all those years ago, with his beautiful paper cutouts and the miracle that happens every time a page is turned, and his ever-present hope for peace.

From Paul's sketchpad in 1939, the year that World War II broke out, when he was thirteen years old

Another drawing from Paul's sketchpad in 1939

This edition published by Kids Can Press in 2019
Originally published in Israel under the title *Hawk and Dove* by Pnina Kor & Kinneret,
Zmora-Bitan, Dvir – Publishing House Ltd.

Kids Can Press gratefully acknowledges the financial support of the Government of Ontario.

Published in Canada and the U.S. by Kids Can Press Ltd.
25 Dockside Drive, Toronto, ON  M5A 0B5

Kids Can Press is a Corus Entertainment Inc. company

www.kidscanpress.com

Designed by Maya Shleifer
English edition edited by Yvette Ghione

Printed and bound in Malaysia, in 10/2018 by Tien Wah Press (Pte.) Ltd.

CM 19  0 9 8 7 6 5 4 3 2 1

**Library and Archives Canada Cataloguing in Publication**

Kor, Pa'ul, author, illustrator
The hawk and the dove / Paul Kor ; translated by Annette Appel.

Translated from the original Hebrew.
ISBN 978-1-5253-0125-4 (hardcover)

I. Appel, Annette (Translator) translator  II. Title.

PZ7.1.K67Ha 2019          j892.43'6          C2018-904115-3